★ THE ADVENTURES OF ★
BeeKLe
The Unimaginary Friend

★ THE ADVENTURES OF ★

BeeKLe

The Unimaginary Friend

Dan Santat

SCHOLASTIC INC.

He was born on an island far away where imaginary friends were created. Here, they lived and played, each eagerly waiting to be imagined by a real child.

Every night he stood under the stars, hoping for his turn to be picked by a child and given a special name.

He waited for many nights.

But his turn never came.

His mind filled with thoughts of all the amazing things that were keeping his friend from imagining him.

So rather than waiting...

...he did the unimaginable.

He sailed through unknown waters
and faced many scary things.

But thinking about his friend
gave him the courage to journey on...

SIR EDMUND HILLARY

...until he reached the real world.

The real world was a strange place.
No kids were eating cake.

No one stopped to hear the music.

And everyone needed naptime.

Then he finally saw something familiar....

So he followed.

He had a good feeling about this place.

But he looked everywhere,

and he could not find his friend.

He climbed to the top of a tree and looked out,
wishing and hoping his friend would come.

But no one came.

He thought about how far he'd come and how long he'd waited, and felt very sad.

Then he heard a noise below.

Hello!

Her face was friendly and familiar, and there was something about her that felt just right.

At first, they weren't sure what to do.

Neither of them had made a friend before.

But...

...after a little while

they realized

they were perfect together.

Beekle and Alice had many new adventures.

They shared their snacks.

COLOR PENCILS

They told funny jokes.

The world began to feel a little less strange.

And together they did the unimaginable.

-for Alek

ABOUT THIS BOOK:
This book was edited by Connie Hsu and designed by David Caplan.
The production was supervised by Erika Schwartz, and the production editor was Christine Ma.

The illustrations for this book were done in pencil, crayon, watercolor, ink, and Adobe Photoshop.
The text was hand-lettered.

ISBN 978-0-545-88091-6

15 16 17 18 19 20/0

12 11 10 9 8 7 6 5 4 3 2

Printed in the U.S.A.

This edition first printing, September 2015

David & Connie

"Beekle!"
—Alek, Age 1